More Adventures with the Purple Crayon

Harold's Trip to the Sky

by *Crockett Johnson*

■ HarperCollins*Publishers*

Copyright © 1957 by Crockett Johnson
Copyright renewed 1985 by Ruth Krauss
All rights reserved. Manufactured in China.
Library of Congress catalog card number: 57–9262
ISBN: 0–06–443025–1 (pbk.)

One night Harold got up, made sure there was a moon so he wouldn't see things in the dark, and went to get a drink of water.

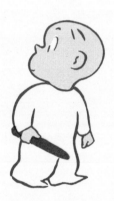

He wondered about the things people see in the dark, and where they came from. He was glad he couldn't see them in the moonlight.

Suddenly he realized he didn't see anything
at all in the moonlight. There was nothing
to see. He was in the middle of a desert.

No wonder he was so thirsty. But, luckily,
he had brought his purple crayon.

And he knew where to find water on a desert.

There was always a pool of it somewhere near
a palm tree.

Harold drank deeply. There is nothing like drinking nice cool water on a desert.

But there isn't much else to do on a desert,
Harold realized as he looked around, except
maybe play in the sand.

Then he remembered how the government has fun on the desert. It shoots off rockets.

Harold decided to go to the moon.

On a good fast rocket, he figured, he could
get there and back in time for breakfast.

He fired the rocket.

And off he went.

But the rocket missed the moon. It missed
it by a mile. And Harold went up and up.

Up and up, he went, into the dark.

Harold tried to see where he was going by
the stars. He tried planets and comets.

What he really needed to light his way was another moon.

But when Harold looked closely, what he
saw wasn't a moon. To his amazement,
it was a flying saucer.

Harold had heard about flying saucers.
People saw them in the dark. And nobody
knew who was inside, flying them.

He decided he had better land his rocket
right away.

He landed it, with a bump, on the bottom
of a strange planet.

There was no danger of falling off so big
a planet.

However, Harold thought he would feel a little more comfortable at the top.

He wondered what planet he was on.

In the dark light of the stars he looked for some sign that might tell him.

He was on Mars.

Harold had heard of men on Mars. So he
yelled a couple of hellos, hopefully.

He thought of the flying saucer out there.
He thought of the things people see in the
dark. He felt a great need for company.

He was sure any man on Mars would be
cordial to a visitor like Harold who had
come all this way to chat with him.

He had to draw on his scanty knowledge of
what a man on Mars looked like.

But his looks wouldn't matter in the dark,
so Harold didn't care much what he turned
out to look like.

All Harold wanted was to know there was
some sort of friendly face close by, even if
he couldn't see it clearly in the dark.

Then, all of a sudden, Harold did see it
clearly. It was the face of a thing.

It was a thing people see in the dark.
And it was sitting in a flying saucer.

Harold ran.

Then he thought and stopped. Probably
the thing was about to fly to earth and
scare somebody, maybe some little child.

Bravely Harold crept back.

He approached on tiptoe, so the thing
wouldn't hear him. And he reached out
with his purple crayon.

And he put a completely damaging crack
in the flying saucer.

Before the thing could grab him he was
off again, chuckling triumphantly.

He ran as fast as he could in the dark.

Happily, most of the way was down hill.

He hoped he wouldn't fall head over heels.

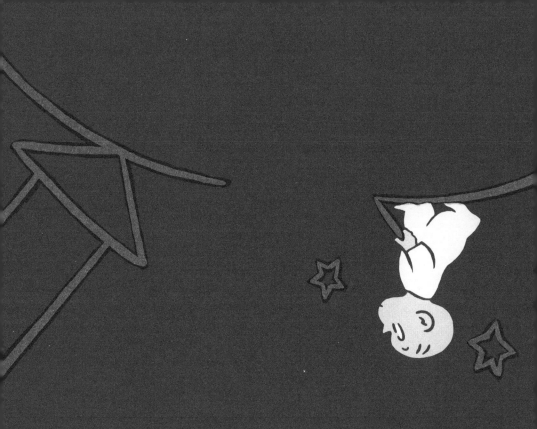

He arrived safely, heels over head, at the
bottom of Mars where the rocket was.

But by this time Harold had had enough
of adventure. He wanted to get home in
a dependable way.

So he climbed down on the stars.

It was sure but slow. And the points of
the stars hurt his feet. Harold wished he
were home.

He recalled that the best way to wish is
on a good big shooting star.

Instead of wishing, it occurred to him at
the last moment to jump aboard.

He shot right down to earth, where he made
a neat two-point landing.

He hadn't passed the moon on the way and
he wondered what had happened to it. It
wasn't anywhere around.

Then he realized the night was just about
gone and it was time for the sun to come up.
He was hungry.

The sun appeared right on time.

It came up big and bright. Harold remarked
that it was going to be a nice day.

Nobody was ever bothered by flying saucers
and things in the sunshine.

But, for a startled moment, he thought he
saw a flying saucer. It was on the horizon,
looking as if it had just come in to land.

He was mistaken. It wasn't a saucer. It
was an oatmeal bowl.

Harold happened to like hot breakfasts.